Katie the kitten

By Kathryn and Byron Jackson
Illustrated by Alice and Martin Provensen

A GOLDEN BOOK • NEW YORK

Katie the Kitten, a small tiger cat,
is asleep in the hall, in a ball, in a hat.

She's awake now. . . .

Just watch her jump up on the chair

to snap at a fly that is buzzing up there!

She chases a dog,

but a very small mouse

can scare Katie the Kitten
right out of the house!

She follows a toad . . .

hippity . . .

hoppity . . .

out by the road.

Katie the Kitten bats at a bee,

and climbs up the trunk
of an old apple tree.

Now she's down.

She boxes her shadow,

and bites her own tail.

She jumps on the table

and falls in the pail.
Poor Katie!

"MEOW!" hear her cry.

She scrambles out quickly,
and shakes herself dry.

She laps her milk neatly,

and eats her fish
with her little front paws
in her pretty red dish.

Katie the Kitten is cozy and fat.

She's back in the hall, in a ball, in a hat.
And she's purring.